I Wish I Was Strong Like Manuel
Quisiera ser fuerte como Manuel

Written by / Escrito por Kathryn Heling and Deborah Hembrook
Illustrated by / Ilustrado por Bonnie Adamson
Translated by / Traducido por Eida de la Vega

For my dear sister Amy, always so strong in spirit!
— KEH
For Troy, love from your other mom.
— Aunt Debbie

For Mollie-dog.
— BCA

Heling, Kathryn and Hembrook, Deborah

I Wish I Was Strong Like Manuel / written by Kathryn Heling and Deborah Hembrook ; illustrated by Bonnie Adamson; translated by Eida de la Vega = Quisiera ser fuerte como Manuel / escrito por Kathryn Heling and Deborah Hembrook; ilustrado por Bonnie Adamson; traducción al español de Eida de la Vega — 1st ed. – McHenry, IL :Raven Tree Press, 2008.

   p. ; cm

Text in English and Spanish.

   Summary: Willie goes to elaborate and comical lengths to be strong like his friend.
      He realizes that he has something that is just as desirable as to be strong.
      Willie gains appreciation of his own uniqueness.

ISBN: 978-0-9770906-7-9 Hardcover
ISBN: 978-0-9770906-8-6 Paperback

   1. Social Situations / Self Esteem & Self Reliance—Juvenile fiction. 2. Social Situations / Friendship—Juvenile fiction.
   3. Boys and Men—Juvenile fiction. 4. Bilingual books—English and Spanish. 5. [Spanish language materials—books.]
   I. Illust. Adamson, Bonnie. II. Title. III. Quisiera ser fuerte como Manuel.

   Library of Congress Control Number: 2007939499

   Printed in Taiwan
   10 9 8 7 6 5 4 3 2 1
   First Edition

I Wish I Was Strong Like Manuel
Quisiera ser fuerte como Manuel

Written by / Escrito por Kathryn Heling and Deborah Hembrook

Illustrated by / Ilustrado por Bonnie Adamson

Translated by / Traducido por Eida de la Vega

Raven Tree Press
A Division of Delta Publishing Company

I wish I was strong like Manuel.
He looks like a super hero!

Quisiera ser fuerte como Manuel.
¡Parece un superhéroe!

4

Manuel and I go to the gym.
I love using the weights. I feel strong!

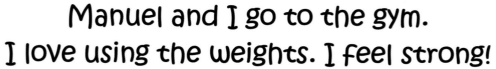

Manuel y yo vamos al gimnasio.
Me encanta levantar pesas. ¡Me siento fuerte!

I wore my brother's water wings
under my sweater.
They made me look like I had muscles.

Me puse los flotadores de mi hermano
debajo del suéter.
Así parecía que tenía músculos.

8

But the air leaked out of one of them.
I'll never do THAT again.

Pero a uno se le escapó el aire.
¡No lo volveré a hacer jamás!

When I play football, I wear shoulder pads.
I pretend they're real muscles.

Cuando juego al fútbol, me pongo las hombreras.
Me imagino que son músculos de verdad.

I wear them all the way home, too!

Me las dejo hasta llegar a casa.

Mr. Miller needed help.
I said I was strong enough to carry the trash.

El señor Miller necesitaba ayuda. Le dije que estaba fuerte y que podía cargar la basura.

What a stinky mess!
I'll never do THAT again!

¡Qué asquerosidad!
¡No lo volveré a hacer jamás!

19

My dad and I stacked firewood.
I tried to carry the heaviest log.

Mi papá y yo apilamos la leña.
Intenté cargar el tronco más pesado.

Ouch!
It fell on my big toe.

¡Ay!
Me cayó en el dedo gordo del pie.

I climbed twelve floors to Grandma's apartment.
I thought my legs would get stronger.

Subí doce pisos hasta el apartamento de la abuela.
Pensé que las piernas se me pondrían fuertes.

But they felt like noodles!
I'll never do THAT again!

¡Pero se me pusieron blandas como fideos!
¡No lo volveré a hacer jamás!

I still wish I was strong like Manuel.

Todavía quiero ser fuerte como Manuel.

But Manuel wishes HE was tall like me.

Pero Manuel quiere ser tan alto como yo.

Imagine that!

¡Imagínate!

30

Vocabulary
English

strong
brother
sweater
muscles
home
trash
firewood
toe
Grandma
legs

Vocabulario
Español

fuerte
el hermano
el suéter
los músculos
la casa
la basura
la leña
el dedo del pie
la abuela
las piernas